I'M BORED

By Michael Ian Black

Illustrated by Debbie Ridpath Ohi

SIMON & SCHUSTER BOOKS FOR YOUNG READERS

New York   London   Toronto   Sydney   New Delhi

I'm bored.

I'm

so

BORED!

What am I supposed to do with **a potato?!!**

I'm bored.

You wanna do something?

Sure.

What do you like to do?

I don't know. **I like flamingos.**

Prove it.

We can turn cartwheels!

Boring.

And skip.

Boring.

Or spin around in circles until we get so dizzy we almost throw up.

Boring.

Kids can

play games

and do ninja kicks

boring,

Boring,

You know what else?

Kids can imagine stuff!

What **kind** of stuff?

Oh, yeah?

Well, now I'm a fairy princess

with my own castle

and dragons

and unicorns

and stuff.

Snoring.

Kids can swing!

Boring.

Kids can jump!

Boring.

Kids can fly!

. Boring.

Boring.

Boring.

Boring.

Boring.

Boring.

Boring.

Hey! A **flamingo!**

Now we can **finally** have some **fun**.

I'm bored.